WHO FLUNG DUNG?

Written and illustrated by

Ben Redlich

meadowside
CHILDREN'S BOOKS

FOR
MY NIECE & NEPHEW,
RACHEL MAY
&
CARL BRANDON REDLICH,
B.R.

First published in 2006
by Meadowside Children's Books
185 Fleet Street
London EC4A 2HS

Text and Illustrations © Ben Redlich
The right of Ben Redlich to be identified
as the author and illustrator has been asserted
by him in accordance with the Copyright,
Designs and Patents Act, 1988

A CIP catalogue record for this book
is available from the British Library

ISBN 10 pbk 1-84539-246-9
ISBN 13 pbk 978-1-84539-246-8
ISBN 10 hbk 1-84539-247-7
ISBN 13 hbk 978-1-84539-247-5

10 9 8 7 6 5 4 3 2
Printed in China

One pleasant day, Furley the monkey
was minding his own business when...

"Who flung dung?"
Furley said, in need of a towel.

No one was around to confess,
so he went to investigate.

After a short while, he saw Elephant and Rhinoceros.

"Who flung dung?"
Furley yelled accusingly.

"Don't look at us!" said Elephant,
"I'd sooner trample you to dust,
than do such a filthy thing!"

"And I'd sooner run at you
and prod you with my nose!"
said Rhinoceros.

"Now, be on your way!"

Furley went on his way.

He soon bumped into
Python and Crocodile.

"Who flung dung?"
Furley screeched at both of them.

"Don't be ridiculous!" said Python, "Even if I could, I wouldn't do such a sorry thing! I'd sooner squeeze you tight and swallow you whole!"

"And I'd sooner snap you up and scoff you down!" said Crocodile. "Now be on your way!"

Furley pushed on in search of the culprit...

Before long he saw Lion.

"Who flung dung?" Furley demanded to know.

"Silly monkey!" said Lion. "Why I'd sooner hunt you down and gobble you up, than do such a horrid thing. Be on your way!"

Just then he saw Vulture and her friends.

"Who flung dung?"
Furley yelled
accusingly.

"Don't be vulgar!" said Vulture.
"We'd sooner pick your bones,
than do such a ghastly thing.
Be on your way!"

On Furley went...

"Who flung dung?"
he cried, again and again.
"Who flung dung?"
"Who flung dung?"

Just then he heard something in the tree.

It sounded like giggling...

It was his brother, Charlie,
looking awfully suspicious.

"You flung dung!"
Furley bellowed knowingly.